For our little ones:
Joey, Morgen, Lucas, Baby Z, and Baby M.
—Eve

◉

Dedicated to those who struggle to find their place in this big world.
Please know you are valuable and destined for greatness.
—Kevin

Text Copyright © 2019 Eve Bunting
Illustration Copyright © 2019 Kevin Zimmer

Sleeping Bear Press™

2395 South Huron Parkway, Suite 200
Ann Arbor, MI 48104
www.sleepingbearpress.com

Printed and bound in China.

10 9 8 7 6 5 4 3 2 1

Library of Congress Cataloging-in-Publication Data

Names: Bunting, Eve, 1928- author. | Zimmer, Kevin (Illustrator), illustrator.
Title: Little yellow truck / written by Eve Bunting; illustrated by Kevin Zimmer.
Description: Ann Arbor, MI : Sleeping Bear Press, [2019] | Summary: A little yellow
pickup truck longs to be included when larger, more powerful vehicles help build
a children's park, but he is soon given a task that is just right for him.
Identifiers: LCCN 2018037159 | ISBN 9781585364077 (hardcover) |
ISBN 9781534110571 (paperback)
Subjects: | CYAC: Trucks—Fiction. | Construction equipment—Fiction. |
Size—Fiction. | Parks—Fiction.
Classification: LCC PZ7.B91527 Li 2019 | DDC [E]—dc23
LC record available at https://lccn.loc.gov/2018037159

Little Yellow TRUCK

By Eve Bunting and Illustrated by Kevin Zimmer

Riley had a red dump truck, a green flatbed truck, a blue concrete mixer, and a little yellow pickup truck at his lumberyard.

One day he told them, "We have an important job to do. I have bought a piece of lumpy, bumpy, clumpy land. Together we will turn it into a beautiful children's park."

Together? An important job? Little Yellow was excited.
He had never been on an important job before.
And never with all the big guys.

Big Blue and Big Red and Big Green and Little Yellow drove to the lumpy, bumpy, clumpy land. Riley and his helpers came too. They picked up the trash and loaded it into Big Red.

Little Yellow watched.

Big Red drove the trash away.

After that, Big Blue turned his big bowl and pumped out concrete.

SQUISH SQUASH SLURP BURP

Riley and his helpers created a picnic area with walkways and a little fountain. They took stacks of lumber that Big Green had carried, and made a fence.

BANG CLANG SMACK WHACK

"Fabulous!" Riley said when they finished.

Little Yellow waited. He flicked his lights on and off.
Don't forget about me! Can't I do something important?

But it was Big Green who drove away with Riley.

It was Big Green who brought the swings and the slides. He brought benches and tables for people to sit on and eat their snacks.

Little Yellow didn't flick on his lights or rumble his engine. The important job was finished and he had done nothing.

Everyone looked all around.

"Fabulous!" Riley said again. "But it's not ready yet."

Little Yellow perked up. **Something for me to do? Something for me?**

"Let's go, Little Yellow," Riley said and climbed behind the wheel.

But it looked as if they were driving back to Riley's lumberyard. Was Little Yellow not going to be part of the children's park after all?

They stopped at Ray's Garden Shop.

Ray's workers began filling Little Yellow with plants and shrubs and flowers. There were bags of soil and grass seed and fertilizer.

THUMP DUMP PLOP DROP

Little Yellow and Riley drove back to the children's park with the sweet smells of jasmine drifting around them.

People waved as they passed.

When they stopped at a red light, a small girl told her mother, "Look! It's a garden in a truck! It's so pretty!"

Riley's helpers scattered the grass seed around the tables and benches. They planted the plants and shrubs and flowers.

"Everything and everyone and every place needs beauty," Riley said. "We're almost ready."

As if by magic, a nice black cloud arranged itself above their little garden and sprinkled it with raindrops.

Butterflies, honeybees, and a hummingbird came to explore.

Riley laughed out loud and said,
"Okay, now we're ready!"

Big Red, Big Green, Big Blue,
and Little Yellow went

HONK   PLONK   HOOT   TOOT

. . . and the children came rushing in.

Riley's helpers cheered, and all the vehicles sounded their horns again.

Little Yellow gave an extra-long

TOOT TOOT TOOTLE TOOT

The children's park was open for business.

And he was part of it!